The Case of the Blazing Star

The Adventures of Shirley Holmes
The Case of the Burning Building
The Case of the Alien Abductions
The Case of the Blazing Star
The Case of the Disappearing Dragon

The Essential Case File

THE CASE OF THE

BLAZING STAR

Screenplay novelisation by
Sue Mongredien

Collins
An imprint of HarperCollinsPublishers

Published in Great Britain by Collins in 1998
Collins is an imprint of HarperCollins*Publishers*Ltd
77–85 Fulham Palace Road, Hammersmith,
London W6 8JB

1 3 5 7 9 8 6 4 2

Created by Winklemania
Original screenplay by Rick Drew
Copyright © Shirley Holmes Productions 1998

ISBN 0 00 675371-X

Printed and bound in Great Britain by
Caledonian International Book Manufacturing Ltd,
Glasgow

THE LEGACY

To the holder of this letter, my commendations.

Solving the puzzle of the chest required more than considerable deductive powers...

My work has consumed my life and I have produced no heir to follow in my path. But I picture you — a young man of good imagination. Any mystery devised by mortal mind can be solved therewith...

Yours faithfully,

Sherlock Holmes

Shirley Holmes would never forget the day she first discovered the secret of the trunk. It had been in the attic for years and most of the time it lay half-forgotten, buried under the usual sort of clutter that no one uses but can't bear to throw away.

From time to time, Shirley would

remember its existence and go and take a look at it. The trunk was a mahogany chest and she enjoyed feeling its intricately carved surface, exploring the patterned grooves of the exotic flora and fauna depicted there. She always wondered what could possibly be inside such an imposing and fascinating receptacle. Her gran didn't know – couldn't even remember where the chest had come from, except that she thought her husband had inherited it from a relative.

The fact that the trunk was locked only roused Shirley's curiosity further, but nobody knew where the key was and it was far too beautiful to break into.

On Shirley's twelfth birthday, the trunk caught her eye again. This time her attention focused on the worn brass plate on the front. On it was etched a series of letters in the Cyrillic alphabet, followed by the numbers: 14551485. It looked like some sort of manufacturer's code, but today's examination of the scratched, metallic surface made Shirley's heart beat faster…

The first thing she noticed was that the letters weren't all Cyrillic – there were also some Arabic and Greek letters. At once Shirley set to work deciphering the letters, which revealed a simple sentence in English: 'Look for clue in 14551485'.

Shirley's mind raced. What could the numbers mean? She tried adding them, multiplying them, organising them in patterns… and then, suddenly, it became clear to her. Pulling down a history book from her shelves she flicked through the pages and a satisfied grin flickered over her face as she read aloud, "1455 to 1485. The

Wars of the Roses. *Yes!*"

But solving one puzzle had only led to another – a scenario that was to become very familiar to Shirley after that day. What on earth could the translation of the message on the brass plate possibly mean? She read the sentence aloud, to see if speaking the words helped in any way.

"Look for clue in the Wars of the Roses."

Furrowing her brow, the girl examined the trunk once more – and discovered an ornate carving of two entwined roses on one side. She ran her fingers along the design – and, suddenly, a latch flipped open. A secret compartment was revealed, inside which was a key...

Holding her breath, Shirley unlocked the chest and raised the heavy lid. She gazed at the contents – not gold or jewels, but it was a unique treasure all the same. Her sharp eyes took in the pile of old diaries and a few musty clothes, the battered violin and a little case containing a pair of gold-rimmed spectacles.

Then she gasped and picked up a deerstalker hat. At once she knew to whom the trunk had belonged – her great-great-uncle, the famous detective Sherlock Holmes.

Shirley knew all about her ancestor. She had apparently inherited his thirst for knowledge, his eye for detail and his ability to solve intricate problems. Somehow, finding her way into this horde of his most private possessions made Shirley feel a true affinity with the man. Instinctively, she also knew that there would be something in the chest that was meant for her.

Carefully rifling through the items,

she passed over ancient relics, glass bottles of foul-smelling liquids and strange, exotic weapons. Finally, tucked into a small shelf in the lid, she discovered the letter…

Avidly, Shirley read the message from beyond the grave. It was definitely written to her – even though Great-uncle Sherlock seemed to think she ought to be a boy.

But if the contents of the letter weren't exactly what she'd been hoping for, they made her determined of one thing: that she would prove a *niece* was just as capable of carrying forth Sherlock Holmes's legacy as a nephew!

Shirley Holmes, detective, was created that day and things were never, ever the same again…

7.00 P.M. REDINGTON STABLES

It was early evening at the Redington Stables and the barn was pretty well deserted. During the day, the stables were always busy and lively, with trainers, jockeys and grooms all working with their horses, but come seven o'clock in the evening it was a different story. The horses were back in their stalls for the night, tired and hungry, and darkness would gather as, one by one, the cars steadily left the car park, homeward bound.

On this night, a single, expensive-looking car purred quietly into the car park, switching off its lights as it pulled up. It was practically the only vehicle there by now. The driver, a Dr Snodgrass, opened his door and went round to the other side to help his passenger, Mrs March, out of the car.

She was the owner of several horses at the stables, and was a familiar figure there – always very well-dressed, but not particularly liked, due to her loud, barking voice, usually to be heard giving instructions or telling someone off!

Dr Snodgrass and Mrs March looked at one another as she stepped out of the vehicle.

"Ready?" she asked, lightly.

He nodded, and they both walked towards the stables.

There were a few stable lights still on as the last horses were being brushed down and settled for the night. Rudy Lamont was one of the jockeys still at work. He was brushing the horse he loved riding best: Blazing Star – a beautiful chestnut with a distinctive white blaze on her forehead. What should have been a straightforward job was taking longer than usual, though, as Blazing Star kept nuzzling at Rudy's jacket pocket, obviously hoping for the treat she knew he usually carried for her.

Rudy laughed and pushed her big head aside. "What are you looking for?" he asked, although he knew very well what the graceful horse was after. She never missed a trick!

"Nope, I don't have any," he told her, as her large brown eyes gazed eagerly into his.

Blazing Star nuzzled at another pocket. She could definitely smell it somewhere...

Rudy continued the brushing and laughed again at his greedy horse.

"Hey, where are your manners?" he scolded, as she nudged him hopefully once more. Blazing Star was a very persistent horse, it had to be said.

It wasn't long before Rudy had to give up pretending. He was never going to get out of here tonight if he didn't give in to her soon!

"OK, OK," he said, pulling out a stick of red liquorice. "Is this what you were after?"

Blazing Star whinnied softly as she gobbled it up and Rudy stroked her nose lovingly as she chewed.

"You are a weird horse, Blazing Star," he said with a smile.

"She was supposed to be ready by now," came a voice at the stable door. Rudy jumped as he turned round to see Tony, one of the stable-hands, standing there expectantly, hands on his hips. There was something about the way he had silently appeared there, as if from nowhere, that made

Rudy shiver.

"Look, I thought I told you to forget it," Rudy said, putting a protective hand on Blazing Star's neck. "I'm not interested in being a part of this!"

Just then, Mrs March and Dr Snodgrass followed Tony into the stable. Mrs March took one look at the horse, then glared at Rudy.

"Last time I checked, I was still the owner of this animal," Mrs March said pointedly.

"But you don't own me," replied Rudy quickly.

Mrs March frowned at him, a sight which terrified the other stable-hands on a regular basis. "This can be as simple, or as difficult, as you want to make it," she told him.

There was a distinctly threatening tone in her voice that gave Rudy the creeps. He stepped closer to Blazing Star, as if trying to protect her, and took hold of her halter.

Mrs March's eyes narrowed at the jockey's action. If that was the way he wanted to play this, then fine! She nodded curtly to Tony, who stepped forward towards Rudy. No one messed with Tony without living to regret it…

CHAPTER 1

"...These trees shall be my books, and in their barks, my thoughts", quoted Mrs Goldstein. *"I'll character that every eye which in this forest looks shall see thy virtue everywhere..."*

It was a hot summer's day at Sussex Academy – so hot, in fact, that Mrs Goldstein had decided to take her English class outside. This was partly because the classroom had been too stuffy and airless to concentrate properly, and partly because it gave her an excuse to wander round barefoot on the grassy school lawn, declaiming her beloved Shakespeare to the class. Mrs Goldstein was a great believer in communing with nature whenever possible – and it was even better if poetry was involved!

"So, class," she continued from under one of the large spreading trees, "what better way to understand Shakespeare's great metaphor than here, in our own natural paradise?"

Stink Patterson groaned quietly. "It's more like hell than paradise," he muttered to his neighbour. He'd already been bitten by something, had suffered ants crawling into his shoes, and now he was being told that this was supposed to be paradise! How anyone could think paradise had the slightest, teeniest link with Sussex Academy was just unbelievable – they'd have to be totally insane, or… or a teacher!

Mrs Goldstein bent down to pick up a stack of papers, then began returning them to their owners.

"By and large, I was very impressed by how inventive your Shakespeare essays were," she told the class warmly. "Such depth of vision, such imagination… and still so young! Well done, all of you!"

Molly Hardy, who had been waiting for the return of her essay with cool confidence, wasn't so enthusiastic about the essays when she saw the mark she'd been given. Molly was usually a straight-A student, always top of the class.

"A-minus?" she read in disbelief. It was probably the lowest mark she'd ever received at this school and she was not happy about it!

To make matters worse, Alicia Gianelli – who was rather more slap-dash in her school work, and had had more than a few Cs in her time – was grinning all over her face.

"I got an A!" she beamed, unable to believe her good fortune.

"There must be some mistake," said Molly smoothly. There, that had wiped the smile off Alicia's face!

Meanwhile, Bartholomew James III – commonly known as Bart – was also smiling at his grade. He glanced over at Stink, who was trying to stuff his essay into his school bag, out of sight!

"Whadya get?" grinned Bart with delight, as he showed Stink his A-grade. It wasn't often he had the chance to go one better over Stink – he might as well milk it!

"English grades are way too subjective!" Stink growled in response, itching to change the subject. How long *was* this lesson going to go on for, anyway?

Mrs Goldstein reached Shirley, and handed over her essay with a warm smile. "Shirley – comparing the character of Caliban to Arnold Schwarznegger…" she began, and then paused. "I loved it!" She winked, and then said conspiratorially, "Most great thinkers can't spell either."

Shirley grinned, pleased with herself, and was about to read the scribbled comments her teacher had written through the essay, when she caught sight of her friend, Bo Sawchuk. He was fast asleep on one of the benches! Sure, it was hot and sunny, but she didn't think Mrs Goldstein would be too thrilled to see that her English class had turned into a sun-napping class!

Uh-oh... it looked like their teacher was on her way over to that part of the lawn right now. Luckily, Molly Hardy had stopped her and was arguing over her grade, so if she acted swiftly enough...

Shirley quickly pulled the ink cartridge out of her biro, crumpled up some paper and pushed it into the casing of her pen. She held it up in Bo's direction, aimed carefully, then fired it through the casing with one powerful breath.

It was a perfect shot!

Bo jumped awake as the missile hit him on the neck, and he gazed around in confusion until he saw

Shirley nodding meaningfully at him, trying to let him know he was about to be rumbled! Bo didn't seem to understand. He was definitely not with-it, and it was only when Mrs Goldstein appeared beside him that he realised what Shirley had been doing.

Mrs Goldstein placed Bo's essay face-down on the grass beside him. "Bo, what happened?" she asked, kindly.

Bo coloured slightly and shrugged, embarrassed at being singled out in front of the class. He knew his essay hadn't been a work of art, sure, but it hadn't been that bad… had it?

"See me after class, OK?" Mrs Goldstein said firmly, and walked on.

Bo flicked up the corner of the essay to check the mark she'd given him, then slumped down on the bench. Great. C-minus. A couple more like that and he would flunk the year if he didn't watch out. He sighed heavily – then straightened up self-consciously as he caught Shirley staring at him with concern in her eyes. Well, one thing was for certain – he didn't want Ace Detective over there poking her nose in to his business!

Knowing Shirley Holmes as he did, though, Bo should have worked out that nothing much could be kept from her if she was interested in finding it out. Even as he was fumbling with his locker combination (what was it again?) when Mrs Goldstein had finally finished with him, there she was behind him.

"It's six left, sixteen right, then twenty-two left," she informed him.

Bo spun around – half-surprised, half-angry. "How do you know my combination number?" he asked.

"Observation," said Shirley with a shrug.

Bo opened his locker door and tossed his English books in. At least *that* lesson was over for another few days! Then he rummaged through his other books and folders, hoping that Shirley would go away if he ignored her long enough.

But Shirley refused to be ignored. "So what did Mrs Goldstein have to say?" she asked.

"Nothing," muttered Bo without looking at her.

"You were in there for twenty minutes," pushed Shirley. She wasn't having any of this 'Nothing' business!

"Yeah," was all Bo answered.

"So?"

Shirley waited for more, but Bo wasn't giving away any extra information. Not one word! He put on his jacket and turned to walk away.

OK, thought Shirley. If he was going to be like that about it...

"Where are you going?" she asked, blocking him.

Bo stared at her, a trace of bitterness in his eyes. "Somewhere no one else in this school goes – to work," he said. "My parents' store – remember? Unlike the rest of the spoiled brats in this school, my family don't get everything handed to them on a plate!"

Shirley was usually sympathetic to the Sawchuk family's financial problems, particularly as Bo was right – most other children who went to Sussex Academy, including herself, had families who were super-rich and never wanted for anything. But there was something about Bo's over-aggressive attitude to her that troubled her. She knew him well enough to know when he wasn't telling her the whole story. So, what was his problem?

"Is that why you quit football?" she asked abruptly before he could leave.

Bo stopped in his tracks and turned towards her, eyes wary. "Who told you that?" he asked suspiciously.

"You did," she replied, noting the sudden relief in his expression. "Usually you come to form period on Mondays and Thursdays, all sweaty from practice. You haven't done that for two weeks." She tapped her nose, and tried a smile at her friend's closed face. "Observation, you see…"

Bo didn't return the smile. He didn't want any more 'observations' from Shirley! Without another word, he walked past her and hurried off down the corridor.

Shirley gazed after him, worried. "Bo…" she called, but either he was pretending not to have heard her, or he genuinely didn't. Whatever the case, in a few seconds he had disappeared around the corner.

Shirley stood in front of his locker after he'd gone. What was wrong with Bo? He was normally so laid-back and fun. Something really had to be troubling him for him to be acting so strangely. Something he didn't want anyone to know about – especially her, it seemed.

Shirley suddenly sniffed at the air.

There had been a distinct smell about Bo as he had left. His jacket, maybe – the smell of it had definitely reminded her of something. She closed her eyes and sniffed again. It was like a farm smell, a country smell – no, a horse smell...

Shirley's eyes snapped open and she glanced both ways up and down the corridor. Well, there was only one way to find out.

Quickly, Shirley turned Bo's combination locker to the correct numbers, then pulled the locker door open, still sniffing. Hmmm. Any clues to be found in here?

Shirley rummaged through various books, Bo's gym bag, a shirt... aha. That smell again. Shirley picked up the shirt, and sniffed once more. *Definitely* a horse smell!

Her eyes flicked curiously around

the open locker for further clues, and then alighted on a piece of straw in a corner. Interesting.

Bo was definitely doing something unusual and the trail was definitely getting warmer...

CHAPTER 2

The Sawchuks' family fish shop was a short walk from school and Shirley decided to pay a quick visit there before she went home. Strike while the iron was hot, and all that – and besides, it was sort of on her way home, after all...

As she entered the shop, Shirley's ears pricked up. Someone was shouting in the back room – and she didn't recognise the voice as belonging to either Mr or Mrs Sawchuk.

"I can't give you more time!" yelled the man's voice threateningly. "Don't even think of asking me again! The rent is the rent, and that's all there is to it!"

Just as Shirley's eyebrows were raising themselves to new heights, a man burst out of the back room of the shop, still shouting. He was short and stocky, dressed in a cheap, grey shiny suit and his face was red with anger. "I'm not running a charity, you know!" he yelled, slamming an envelope down on the counter. The shop door banged shut behind him as he left.

Shirley carefully placed her school bag on the counter, covering the letter as Mr and Mrs Sawchuk emerged from the back room. They both looked distressed by the argument, although as soon as they spotted Shirley there, they smiled weakly at her in an attempt to hide their feelings.

"Shirley," said Mrs Sawchuk pleasantly. "How are you?"

"Hi, Mrs Sawchuk, Mr Sawchuk," said Shirley, smiling back. "Can I talk to Bo, please?"

"He's still at football practice," his mum told her, wiping her hands on her apron.

Football practice? But... Oh, right. Bo wasn't at football practice (which she knew already) and he wasn't at home either... It didn't take a genius to figure he must be doing something else – something he was keeping secret from both Shirley *and* his parents. Shirley had to backtrack.

She didn't seem to be in Bo's good books anyway, at the moment – so she certainly didn't want to make it any worse by dropping him in it with his parents!

"Oh yeah, of course," she said, casually. "I forgot. I'll see him later."

Time to get out of there! Then, still thinking on her feet, Shirley scooped up her school bag from the counter, making sure she also scooped up the letter the red-faced man had left behind. The Sawchuks watched her leave and then went back into the other room once more. They had a lot to talk about...

Outside the shop, Shirley pulled out a can of hairspray from her bag. It sure paid off to be well-prepared in the detective business! She popped the top off the can and gave the letter a good spraying all over. Desperate times called for desperate measures, after all! Although she wasn't particularly enjoying snooping into Bo's private family business like this, she did want to help her friend. That meant she'd do whatever she had to do, however unpleasant.

Shirley peered at the envelope as the hairspray soaked through the paper and made it transparent. Then she peered again. The message inside was becoming horribly clear: **EVICTION NOTICE** it read in large, bold lettering.

Shirley waved the envelope dry, shocked at its contents. Evicted! Were the Sawchuks so badly in debt that they were going to be evicted? What on earth could she do to help? Did Bo know about it? Shirley guessed that he did, which explained his hostility and depression. He'd probably got a second job which meant that he worked late *every* night after school. If that were so, he'd only half-lied to Shirley. And no wonder he was falling asleep in lessons from tiredness.

Shirley gazed thoughtfully at the envelope as the hairspray evaporated and its appearance returned to normal once more. She glanced in through the shop window and, seeing that the coast was clear, sneaked quietly in and left the envelope on the front counter, just as she'd found it. As she was leaving, she heard Bo's parents talking in the back room in worried voices.

"It'll work out. It always does," Mr Sawchuk was saying firmly.

His wife sounded as if she was in tears. "No!" she said. "Mother of God, we have to do something!"

"We'll try the bank again," Mr Sawchuk said, trying to comfort her, although he didn't sound too convinced himself. "I'll explain to them! I'll make them understand!" He paused, and Shirley thought she heard a sob from Mrs Sawchuk.

"You'll see, everything will be OK," promised her husband.

Shirley sighed as she walked on towards home. Why did everything have to be so difficult? Why couldn't everyone just be happy and have enough money to do all the things they wanted? Surely enough money for people to be able to pay their rent wasn't too much to ask for?

A flicker of guilt passed through her as she opened the front door of her large, comfortable home. It just wasn't fair!

CHAPTER 3

Bo, meanwhile, was unaware of the latest developments at the fish shop. He was hard at work mucking out one of the stalls at Redington Stables, where he'd been employed to work after school. He was hot and tired and seriously in need of a drink, but then the horse in the next stall whinnied softly to him, and he turned, smiling at her. Blazing Star –

his favourite horse. There were definitely some parts of the job that made the rest of the hard work all worthwhile.

"And what do you want?" he asked affectionately. "As if I didn't know!"

Bo dug a liquorice stick out of his pocket – it had been a regular work accessory, the bag of red liquorice sticks. Everyone knew that Blazing Star had a real taste for it!

This time, however, Blazing Star didn't seem so interested in the red stick Bo held out to her. Instead of munching at it straightaway as she usually did, she turned her head away and ignored what was normally her favourite treat.

Bo frowned. "What's your problem?" he asked her, puzzled. "Go on – take it! You love liquorice, silly!"

"Can't be good for a horse's teeth..." came a voice from behind him.

Bo turned around, recognising the speaker's voice. Well, well – what a surprise. Ms Holmes herself, back for some more snooping. Bo could barely keep the annoyance out of his voice.

"What are you doing here?" he asked rudely.

"Simple deduction," said Shirley, undeterred. "After I noticed the smell of horse barn on your shirt, I..."

Bo stared at her, and then held up a hand to stop her. "Wait a minute," he said. "What shirt?"

"The shirt in your locker," was the frank reply.

Bo's eyes grew wide in disbelief.

"You broke into my locker?" he asked incredulously. "You *broke* into my *locker*?"

Shirley shrugged, seemingly unruffled by Bo's angry expression. "Yeah," she said simply. "And I went to the fish shop looking for you. Don't worry," she continued, as Bo's mouth dropped open, "I covered for you." Shirley looked Bo square in the eyes. "So, did you get a second job here to help out your parents?"

Bo folded his arms across his chest, eyes narrowing with anger. "Hang on," he said, sarcastically. "You're saying that you went snooping around my stuff, and…"

Bo broke off suddenly as one of the jockeys entered the stall. He looked apologetically at Bo as he noticed the tension in the air.

"Am I interrupting something?"

he asked.

Bo was about to reply when he caught sight of the painful-looking black eye on the right side of the jockey's face. "Rudy!" he exclaimed, coming over to take a closer look. The bruising was pretty nasty. "What happened to you? Did you have a fall?"

Rudy seemed sheepish as he crossed over to Blazing Star and put a lead on her halter. His eyes were on the lead rather than Bo and Shirley as he answered.

"It was my own fault," he said, shrugging. "I was mounting her, and Blazing Star whipped her head back and nailed me a good one." He gave the horse an affectionate pat on the neck. "Weird creature!"

Shirley decided it was high time she made herself known to the jockey. She never liked being left out of anything! She stepped forward confidently. "Hi," she said to Rudy.

Rudy looked at her, and then at Bo, obviously expecting a proper introduction. Just as Shirley had predicted! Sighing, Bo gave it to him.

"Rudy, this is Shirley," he said wearily.

Rudy smiled at her. "Hi," he said back.

"Is she your horse?" asked Shirley, coming closer still. Not a mad keen horse-fan herself, she was nevertheless impressed by the fine chestnut beast in front of her.

"Unfortunately not," said Rudy. "I just ride her. But I was with her when she was born – and just about every minute of her life since then, so you could say she and I know one another pretty well."

He smiled at the horse's large intelligent face. "Anyway, I'll leave you to it," he said quickly, remembering that he had walked in on what had seemed like a tense moment. "See you later, Bo!"

As Rudy led the horse out of the stall, he looked at the pair of them curiously, wondering if Shirley was Bo's girlfriend. He'd known Bo and the Sawchuk family for years, but Bo had never mentioned Shirley to him. Whatever, it was perfectly clear that the two of them had been having a row when he'd arrived... and he certainly didn't want to be around when they were finishing it off!

The moment he was out of earshot, Shirley turned triumphantly to Bo. "Blazing Star didn't give him that black eye," she said firmly.

"What do you mean? You heard

what he said, didn't you?" asked Bo.

"That bruise was on the right side of his face," Shirley replied. "Horses are always mounted from the left side."

Bo shot her a scathing look and carried on with his mucking-out. He had had just about enough of Shirley's detective work for one day... she seemed to think it was all one big mystery game, when in fact it was actually his life she was interfering with all the time. Friends weren't supposed to do that to each other, whether they were detectives or not!

Shirley caught sight of Bo's face and felt a little awkward. "Just observation," she muttered, knowing full well what he thought of her observations that day.

There was a moment's heavy

silence. Bo carried on steadily mucking out, ignoring Shirley completely and hoping she would get the hint and go away.

Shirley hesitated – should she tell Bo what she'd seen at the fish shop, or not? She decided to go for it, and plunged right ahead.

"Bo," she began nervously, watching his face carefully, "your parents... your parents got an eviction notice today."

Bo recoiled as if he'd been slapped. He was obviously hugely shocked at this bit of news and stared Shirley full in the face for several seconds. She dropped her eyes, unable to look at his expression. Then he suddenly pushed roughly past her, out to the racing track where Shirley's bike was leaning against a fence-post.

Shirley trailed after him, reluctant

to leave, but knowing that Bo was in no mood for company. Perhaps she should have kept her mouth shut about the eviction notice after all…

Bo stood by Shirley's bike and glared at her. "I'm going to tell you what's going on, and then you're going to lay off me," he said. The way he said it left no room for any discussion of the matter.

"I accept your terms – provisionally," said Shirley after a moment's thought. The mood Bo was in, it was definitely going to be a safer option to agree with whatever he said right now.

"First, get on your bike," he told her.

Shirley did so, then looked back at him expectantly.

Bo leaned against the fence-post, as if all the fight had suddenly gone out of him.

"OK," he said slowly, tracing a finger along the grain of the wood. "Basically, it's my uncle. He's back in the Ukraine. Things are tough there and sometimes my parents help him out. This time, he couldn't pay us back."

"So that's why you got this job – to help them pay the rent?" prompted Shirley.

Bo nodded. "Yeah. And my parents would flip if they knew I was working here." His voice turned cold and he folded his arms across his chest. "So that's the big mystery," he said sarcastically. "Exciting, wasn't it? I bet you're glad you went to all that trouble snooping around to find that out." He paused, and glared at her. "Now scram, like you promised," he said.

Shirley didn't catch the glare on his face, though. She was watching something behind Bo's shoulder – Rudy on the training track with Blazing Star. Although Shirley was no expert on racehorses, Blazing Star didn't seem to be behaving very well for her rider – she kept pulling her head to the side, rearing up and making silly little prancing steps.

The whole performance was being watched by an oldish man with a briefcase and a middle-aged woman, who were both leaning over the fence.

"Easy! Easy, Star!" Rudy kept calling, but it didn't seem to make any difference.

"I thought he grew up with that horse," Shirley mused.

Bo's reply was to point towards the driveway.

"Shirley," he said in exasperation, "this one's not a game, remember? This is not some silly mystery to write up in your journal. This is my life. No detective work here, OK? And the gate's that way."

He turned back towards the barn, adding a muttered, "See you tomorrow," over his shoulder as he walked away.

"OK," said Shirley softly. She could tell Bo had had more than enough of her for one day, and he was right – it was his life she was snooping about in. But she couldn't help wondering a little, because things weren't quite adding up…

On her way out of the grounds, Shirley made sure she passed close by the training track. Blazing Star was still playing up, turning round and round, and jerking Rudy about on her back. She heard the concern in Rudy's voice as he called over to the man by the fence.

"She's real skittish, Dr Snodgrass."

"That's to be expected," came the reassuring reply. "She'll settle down in time."

Dr Snodgrass, eh? Why would a doctor be around? Shirley hadn't heard any mention of Blazing Star being anything other than in peak condition – but why had she been playing up lately? Rudy's black eye... her skittish behaviour on the track... Bo hadn't known anything about having to see a doctor – and Rudy hadn't mentioned it either, but the horse *did* seem to be acting out of character.

The doctor put something in his bag. "See you later!" he called, leaving Rudy alone with Blazing Star.

Shirley slowed her bike right down and watched as the doctor left the training track and got into his car. DR NED SNODGRASS, VETERINARY SURGEON read a sign on the car door. Gotcha!

Shirley noted down the doctor's full name and watched as the car pulled away. She had a hunch something strange was going on at the race track, but she still couldn't quite put her finger on exactly what it was. Shirley thought hard as she cycled home. Well, whether there was anything peculiar happening or not, she would find out – or her name wasn't Shirley Holmes!

CHAPTER 4

Shirley didn't see Bo until the next morning when she stumbled upon a very strange scene at school.

As she walked down the corridor to her form-room, there, hanging from the string of a helium balloon which was pressing itself against the ceiling, was a pair of large gym shorts. Uh-oh. Someone was in trouble...

Shirley pushed her way through the crowd, curious to find out what was going on. Bart, Molly, Bo and Stink were all standing around laughing… as was Alicia. Only she wasn't laughing. She was staring up at the shorts with horror, and then checking her locker frantically, hoping the airborne shorts just looked like hers.

No such luck. They were hers.

"That's probably funny on your planet," she said witheringly to Stink. You didn't have to be a great detective to clock that this was exactly the kind of stupid stunt he would pull.

"Hey, I'm as innocent as the day I was born!" he protested, holding his hands out and grinning.

"That doesn't say much!" growled Alicia. She put her hands on her hips.

"Now get them down!"

Stink wasn't moved by Alicia's fierceness. "I can't, I'm afraid," he said casually, swaggering off. "But don't worry, the helium'll leak out in about a week, or maybe the cleaners will get them down when they're here at the weekend..."

Alicia gritted her teeth. "Kill me if I ever go on another date," she muttered to Molly. "Or even talk to a boy! They're a different species!"

Molly smiled, almost looking sympathetic. Shirley knew, however, that no one would ever dare pull a stunt like that on Molly Hardy. *She'd* have eaten the culprit for breakfast!

Shirley watched as Bo walked up, pulled the balloons down and passed Alicia's gym shorts back to her. She clutched them tightly, and beamed at him. "Thanks, Bo!"

Molly looked at Alicia in amusement. "Do I get to kill you now or later?" she asked sweetly.

"Oh, Bo doesn't count," Alicia replied, stuffing her shorts back in her bag.

Bo just rolled his eyes at that. He seemed to be in a much better mood, Shirley noted with relief. In fact, he seemed almost like his old, jokey self. Perhaps he was even in an approachable mood today, and maybe she wouldn't get her head bitten off…

"Multiple personalities," she said, going over to him with a small smile. "The only explanation for your mood swings."

Bo beamed at her, and leant in conspiratorially. He *was* in a better mood! Almost as if he didn't have a care in the world.

"No," he said confidently. "I've got a great way of saving my parents' shop… and I'm going to do it!"

Shirley raised her eyebrows. This Bo was rather a different one from yesterday! Were body-snatchers in town, or something? "That's great," she said slowly. "How?"

They started walking along the corridor together. "It's so cool," Bo told her, happily. "I'm going to clean up on a big horse race this weekend. I'm betting all my money on Blazing Star, no less! She's going to win me a fortune!"

Shirley looked at him curiously. "You're making a bet?" she asked in surprise. "But you're not old enough."

Bo shrugged airily. Being old enough was not exactly his most pressing concern right now. "A friend's placing it for me," he answered.

"Rudy?" guessed Shirley, but for once her deductions were wrong.

"No – he can't bet, because he's riding," Bo explained. "He's racing Blazing Star, isn't he? That little gold mine! The odds are 12-1 against her, but Rudy's sure she's going to win. So at 12-1, I stand to make a tidy packet..."

Shirley frowned. "How can he be so sure Blazing Star will win?" she asked cautiously.

"Rudy knows that horse," Bo assured her. "Honestly, Shirley, it's a dead cert!"

But Shirley was thinking of the Blazing Star she'd seen – skittish and inattentive, and giving her jockey a black eye. "Nothing's a dead cert," she said slowly. "That's why they call it gambling."

Bo's face darkened and his shoulders slumped. "Why can't you just be happy for me?" he said fiercely. "Why do you have to put a damper on everything? I'm trying to help my parents, you know – my parents, who – unlike your father – don't work in an Embassy and don't have tax-free salaries and big mansions!"

Ouch! Bo's face was stony as he walked away, but Shirley hadn't finished the conversation. "Bo – what if Rudy's cheating?" she called after him urgently. For the second time in as many days, Bo ignored her and walked away, hands in his pockets.

Shirley sighed. Everything kept going wrong between her and Bo. He was so touchy about everything she said to him these days. She had to admit, she knew her interfering in his affairs was bugging him – to say the least! – and she knew he hadn't wanted her to doubt his get-rich-quick plan, as she had. But he was her friend! Friends were *meant* to interfere now and again! And she owed it to him to interfere as long as she suspected foul play. In the case of Blazing Star, it did seem as though there was some information that she just wasn't getting to hear about. Like – why would Rudy say Blazing Star was a dead cert to win, when clearly she wasn't?

Shirley decided to consult her gran that night. Grandma was the wisest, cleverest person Shirley knew and was usually good for shedding light on a baffling problem.

As it happened, the opportunity couldn't have been better. Grandma needed to hand in a piece of work for her still-life painting class... what better model could there be than her granddaughter?! And that meant Shirley had Grandma all to herself for the evening... time for a few questions!

Shirley had a vague idea how the betting system in horse-racing worked but she was delighted to find that Grandma seemed to know all about it.

"So if a horse is running at 12-1, that means that someone putting a one-dollar bet on it, would win twelve dollars if the horse won?" she asked.

"Correct!" Grandma answered, mixing up a little white paint. "Although those are fairly high odds," she went on, "which means the horse wouldn't necessarily be brilliant."

"Right." Shirley took this in. "So for a horse to have high odds... would that mean that it had probably lost a lot of races?"

"That's right." Grandma smiled at the serious expression on Shirley's face. "Why the sudden interest in gambling, darling? Don't tell me you're going to start spending your pocket money at the races?"

"It's something for school," Shirley answered, crossing her fingers out of sight. She decided to go on with her line of questioning before Grandma could ask any more awkward questions in return. "Anyway. What were we saying...? Oh yeah, so if a horse is *that* bad, why would anyone want to bet on him?"

"Think of the mathematics,"

Grandma told her. "The higher the risk, the greater the pay-off. Some gamblers love big odds." She put her paintbrush down suddenly, and her eyes took on a faraway look.

"Imagine putting down your last hundred dollars on a horse that's a hundred-to-one," she said passionately. "Think how it would feel watching that horse pummel down the home stretch, neck and neck with just one other. In a single stride, that horse could make you rich, or could leave you penniless." She sighed. It seemed to be an effort for her to return to the real world. "It's that very instant many people live for," she finished up, raising her eyebrows knowledgeably at her granddaughter.

Shirley wasn't swayed by the romance Grandma seemed to see in gambling and horse-racing. She was far too practical for that!

"Uh-huh," she said, rather dismissively. "But Gran, if a jockey says he's sure he's going to win... would he be fixing the race, do you think?"

Grandma shrugged. "Usually you fix it by deliberately losing. That clears the way for another horse to win. And that's the one you bet on." She frowned, picking up the paintbrush once more. "Of course, there's always steroids too," she added disapprovingly.

Shirley's face lit up. Steroids! Of course. She hadn't thought about that. Perhaps that would explain why the veterinary surgeon had been down at the training track the other day...

CHAPTER 5

The very next day, Shirley decided to pay Dr Snodgrass a visit. His office was very close to the training track, and easy enough to find. However, she wasn't able to get to his surgery until after school that afternoon – and only then, once she'd cycled home to collect Watson, her faithful basset hound and the perfect accomplice.

By the time she had cycled back to

the doctor's surgery it was almost five o'clock and Dr Snodgrass was about to close up.

Shirley decided to opt for the silly-little-girl approach. It always seemed to fool middle-aged guys (apart from Dad, unfortunately). As Dr Snodgrass turned to leave his office, he found Shirley blocking his path with Watson in her arms.

"I know you're a horse doctor," began Shirley plaintively, "but my doggy got some straw in his eye and I'm worried that he's in real big pain."

The vet barely glanced at her – he was too busy looking at his watch. "Sorry, dear," he said, "I'm due at the track any minute. Another time, hmmm?"

Shirley hated being called dear at the best of times, let alone when the person in question was ignoring her into the bargain! She stepped the silly-little-girl approach up a gear...

"Look, his eye's all red," she wailed, sticking out her bottom lip slightly for added effect. "Please, please, please won't you help? His name's Watson..."

Dr Snodgrass sighed and put down his briefcase. He took Watson from Shirley's arms and put him on the examining table for a closer look. Shirley pushed up close next to him and carried on talking.

"He's a basset hound, you know," she said chattily. "I wanted a bloodhound really, but my dad said they grow too big, and our yard is pretty small. Basset hounds are fine too, though. Have you ever seen them run? They look so funny! And did you know Shakespeare compared them to Thessalian bulls?"

She paused for breath and Dr Snodgrass seized the chance to get away from her incessant babble. He couldn't concentrate with that endless chat! "Er... why don't you just wait here?" he asked quickly.

Shirley hid a grin as she nodded. It was just what she'd wanted to hear!

Dr Snodgrass picked up Watson and disappeared into his examining room. As soon as he had shut the door behind him, Shirley went over to the filing cabinets and, quick as a flash, started rifling through the papers in the drawer marked 'Animals: A-D'. Would Blazing Star be under B as her initial, or H for Horse?!

B... B... B... Aha – this folder was marked 'Blazing Star'. Bingo! She took out her camera-pen and snapped a picture of each form inside the file.

Then she heard Watson bark and the door of the examining room swing open, and she quickly closed the file again. Perfect!

Dr Snodgrass reappeared, looking irritated. He set Watson down on the table. "There's nothing wrong with this animal," he said briskly. "Red eyes are characteristic of this breed."

Watson thumped his tail in agreement and Shirley pretended to look amazed at this information. "They are?" she asked in mock-surprise. "Fancy that! Well, come on, Watson, there's nothing wrong with you after all!"

She hurried out of the surgery before the annoyed vet could see the grin that now covered her face. As they walked past the stables, Watson started tugging stubbornly at the lead. He had smelled something – someone – familiar!

"Hey, Watson, c'mon," Shirley coaxed, but he was too eager to be stopped by his owner. With one swift movement, he tore the lead out of Shirley's hand and took off towards the nearby horse barn.

Scooting through the entrance, Watson barked joyfully as he recognised a friend.

"Watson?" Bo had been moving bales of hay around inside one of the stalls and was surprised to see the small four-legged animal bounding in to see him. Dogs always seemed such small animals when you were working with horses all day!

Bo turned around quickly. If Watson was there, it could only mean that... Shirley was too. Not again!

Sure enough, she soon appeared in the stall with a guilty expression on her face. This time, she had planned to collect her information without bugging Bo about it – in fact, she'd been hoping to get out of there without seeing him at all. Now it was too late!

Bo sighed heavily. "Oh, man…" he started, but Shirley plunged ahead before he could get angry.

"I know I promised to leave you alone, Bo…" she started, but this time he interrupted.

"Doing a good job of it so far, obviously, Shirley," he retorted sarcastically.

Shirley couldn't bear having her friend treat her so coldly, but there were things she had to know. "Bo, why did Rudy lie to you about his black eye?" she burst out. "And why has Blazing Star been acting up?"

Bo glanced over at the chestnut horse, who was standing calmly in the next stall. "She hasn't," he said. "You don't know what you're talking about, Shirley Holmes!"

Shirley hadn't finished, though. "Why is a horse that's finished last five times in a row suddenly expected to win a race?"

Bo was defensive. "She had a bad leg, but it's healed now. Rudy's been holding her back," he said, then added rudely, "Not that it's anything to do with you."

"What if he'd been giving her steroids?" Shirley pressed.

Bo shook his head, dismissing the idea straightaway. "No way!" he said. "He's not giving her steroids!" He turned away from Shirley to pick up a large hay bale. He'd just about had enough of this…

"Steroids increase aggression," Shirley argued. "That would explain why Rudy's having a hard time handling her…"

She was interrupted at that moment by an angry snort from Blazing Star, almost as if the horse was joining in the argument. Shirley and Bo both looked around quickly to see what was wrong with her, only to see Watson nosing around in her stall.

"Watson! Here, boy!" called Shirley, not liking the sound of the snort.

"It's OK," Bo told her. "Star likes dogs."

Shirley wasn't so sure about that! Watson barked at the horse and the very next second, Blazing Star was rearing up at the dog, neighing loudly, nostrils flared.

Bo tried to grab hold of her halter. "It's OK, girl!" he called comfortingly – but the horse wasn't having any of it! She neighed again, kicking out frantically. "Whoa!" he cried.

Shirley leant forward quickly and yanked Watson's lead, dragging him out. Those hooves were going all over the place and she didn't want to have to go to Dr Snodgrass for a genuine injury to her dog!

"Thought you said she liked dogs," she remarked.

The horse really didn't seem to like them at all! Now Blazing Star was getting hysterical, even though Watson had been removed. She reared up at Bo, who was white with shock, and trapped him against the wall. Her powerful legs kicked up only centimetres away from his face and Bo held his breath, staring at the nervous horse in terror.

"Star!" he yelled, his voice cracking in fright. "Easy, girl! Easy!"

Luckily, his cries were enough to alert help. Rudy, Tony and Mrs March all heard the noise and rushed in to see what was happening. Rudy grabbed the horse's halter and began calming Blazing Star down, whispering soothing words into her ears, while keeping a firm hold of her trembling neck.

While the horse was occupied, Bo managed to slip out of the stall unhurt and leant against the wall, panting and looking faintly green.

Mrs March was furious. "I ought to fire you!" she yelled at Bo. "Blazing Star could have been hurt! Bringing your dog into the stables like that!"

Shirley pushed poor Watson out of

the way. "He's my dog," she told the angry woman.

For her honesty, she was rewarded by a furious glare from Mrs March. "And who are you?"

"It's no big deal," Rudy said pointedly, before Shirley could answer. All heads turned to him, at the firm note in his voice. "Star likes dogs... remember?"

He gave Mrs March a long look which seemed to say more than his actual words had.

She hesitated a second, then turned back to Shirley. "Get out," she said coldly. "And if I see you on these premises again, I'll call security."

Shirley set her jaw. There didn't seem to be much point arguing with this furious woman, although she couldn't help wondering what had been meant by the look that had passed between her and Rudy.

Mrs March seemed to have dismissed her, though. She was now concentrating on Bo. "As for you, I expect a day's work for a day's pay!" she told him fiercely.

Shirley decided to make a quick exit, with Watson in tow, before either of them got yelled at again. It was worse than being at school, all this shouting and telling off!

As she turned to leave, she spotted a large, fragrant pile of fresh horse droppings outside Star's stall. Here went nothing…

She trod into the pile of droppings with a squelch. The things you had to do as a detective these days! "Yuck," she muttered to herself, hoping that this was going to be worth the effort. It had better be! She limped out of the barn and round the corner, out of sight. There she stopped, took off the offending boot and dropped it on the ground beside her. Balancing on one leg, she took a plastic bag out of her backpack, ready to scrape a sample of the horse droppings into it.

"Evidence," she told Watson seriously, who was already giving it a good sniff.

But before she could start scraping, the boot was grabbed out of her hand. Bo had caught her red-handed! (Or bare-footed, she mentally corrected herself.)

"That's what I think of your stupid evidence," he told her, tossing the boot far away over the field, as far as he could.

Shirley stared at him. "Bo…" she began helplessly.

But Bo didn't want to hear anything from her right then. "Stop treating me like a specimen you've put under your microscope!" he yelled at her. "There's no mystery here – just my life. My life, as I keep telling you! Why can't you just leave me alone?!"

There was a second or two of silence following Bo's outburst, and Shirley felt awful. She really was upsetting him.

"I'm worried about you," she told him honestly. For it was true – she was worried. She'd never seen him so uptight and angry before.

Bo gave a sarcastic laugh. "You've got a funny way of showing it," he told her. "You almost got me killed! And then almost got me fired! Good work, Ms Holmes. Elementary!"

He turned and left, leaving Shirley still balancing awkwardly in the mud. She waited until he'd gone and then, in a low voice, said "Fetch!" to Watson. Bo or no Bo, she'd get to the bottom of this case... but before she could do anything, she needed her boot back!

CHAPTER 6

That night, Shirley set about developing the photographs she'd taken of Dr Snodgrass's file on Blazing Star. As Grandma was a keen photographer also, Shirley knew how to use the darkroom herself and it didn't take her long to have the photographs developed and drying on a line.

While she waited for the pictures

to dry, she tested the sample of horse droppings she'd taken from her boot. Shirley had a keen interest in science and her father had set up a mini-laboratory for her one year, as a Christmas present. Whenever she sat at her desk, surrounded by bottles of liquid, papers and various pieces of chemistry equipment, Shirley really felt like a scientist. Especially when she was wearing her white lab coat!

She stared at the results in the test tube, disappointment in her eyes. "No steroids," she muttered to herself, noting the clear liquid. So that was *that* theory down the drain. Shame…

Sighing in frustration, Shirley crossed the steroid idea out of her notebook. Well, if it wasn't steroids, what was it that was causing Blazing Star to act so strangely? Shirley picked up her soiled boot once more, and stared at the sole, hoping for inspiration. She wrinkled her nose in disgust. Come on, all she wanted was a little clue... anything!

She peered in closely at something she'd just spotted, stuck in with the rest of the muck. With tweezers she carefully pulled it out: a single oat. Shirley frowned.

Oats. That rang a bell somewhere...

Pulling out her magnifying glass, Shirley examined one of the photos that was hanging up to dry – Blazing Star's medical record. It was a form with various boxes checked and notes filled in here and there: distinguishing marks, allergies, previous illnesses, and as Shirley scanned down the photograph, she began to smile. Just as she had remembered! In the allergies section, the word 'oats' had a ring around it.

If Blazing Star was allergic to oats, what was she doing eating them? Could the way she had been behaving really be an allergic reaction – or was there something more to it?

Next day at the stables, Bo was working hard as usual when he caught sight of Rudy with Blazing Star. Rudy looked tired and stressed out, and Bo stopped what he was doing to gaze at him with concern. Rudy was usually so carefree and full of life! But he seemed to have lost all his energy lately, for some reason.

Bo called over to him. "Rudy!"

Rudy turned and gave him a half-smile, although it didn't get quite as far as his eyes. "Not now, Bo, I've got to go to the gym," he said, still walking.

Bo grinned at him warmly, trying to encourage him. "Great! Keep it up, champ – I'm betting on you in the race, you know!"

Rudy stopped, looked back at his friend and came over to Bo, a worried look on his face. "What did you say?" he asked.

"The race," Bo repeated, giving Blazing Star a friendly pat. "I'm putting down all my money on you two – I'm counting on you both!"

Rudy bit his lip, and said nothing.

Bo was confused. "What? There's no risk, is there?" he asked, sounding unsure. "Why are you looking like that? I mean, you said so yourself… " His words tailed off into nothing.

Rudy sounded cross when he finally replied. "Yeah, well, it's just that I don't think it's such a good idea, you getting involved in betting. You're only a kid, Bo – what would your parents think?"

Bo was taken aback. This wasn't the response he'd been expecting from his friend. He was only trying to support him – and himself!

"Well, they would think it was pretty great if I won enough money to stop them being evicted," he said slowly, his eyes fixed on Rudy. Then a sudden irritable twitch from Blazing Star as he patted her again made him turn to the horse.

"What's wrong with you, anyway?" Bo asked her. "I don't know who's crankier these days," he continued, speaking to Rudy now, "you or Star! Neither of you have been yourselves at all lately! Both of you are being funny with me – it's enough to make a guy paranoid!"

Rudy started at the criticism. He watched Bo with the horse and felt guilty for his harsh words.

"You're really starting to learn about horses," he told him in a softer voice. "You're starting to feel what she's feeling. That's good." He smiled at Bo, anxious to make up for his bad mood. "Be nice to her though, eh. She's got a race to run, you know!"

Bo smiled back, the outburst forgotten. "She's got a race to win, you mean."

CHAPTER 7

By the time the race actually came round a week later, Shirley Holmes reckoned she'd just about pieced together all the pieces of the Blazing Star puzzle. There was only one thing missing... concrete proof. And where better to get it than on the horse itself? But first she had to get through all the security, as well as past the dreadful Mrs March, to be able to check her facts for sure.

As all great detectives, Shirley had come well-prepared. She bided her time outside the jockeys' changing room, then, when all the jockeys seemed to have left in their brightly coloured silks, she figured the coast was pretty much clear and snuck right in there.

Shirley found a pair of jodhpurs, a jockey's riding hat and goggles, and quickly dressed in them, tying her hair up and hiding it underneath the hat. She had a quick look in the long mirror and grabbed a riding crop for good measure. Would she pass as one of the jockeys dressed like this? She certainly hoped so!

Shirley left the changing room without wasting any further time and set off in the direction of the stables. She had a brief moment of panic when she spotted Mrs March and Tony approaching, but she pulled her hat slightly lower, kept her head well down and strode purposefully past them. If in doubt, look as if you know what you're doing, she reminded herself. It never usually failed!

Sure enough, apart from a curious sideways look from Mrs March at the strange jockey she didn't recognise, Shirley managed to pull it off and made her way to the stables without being questioned once.

Now came the tricky bit. According to Grandma, the only true way to identify a horse was by its registration tattoo. The only question was... where was Blazing Star's tattoo?

Shirley gulped as she eyed the powerful-looking racehorse. She slunk nervously into the stall, remembering the frenzied horse she'd seen nearly kicking Bo to pieces the other day. Good one, Shirley. Now she was alone with the same horse, and had to find a number tattooed on its body. No problem… in her dreams!

Blazing Star snorted suspiciously at the approaching stranger. Shirley tried to soothe her, as she'd seen Rudy do. "I… er… hello," she said uncertainly. "I'm just going to look for a tattoo which… um… says who you are."

She paused. Now that she was up close to the horse, she realised just how big Blazing Star really was. She was bigger than big – she was *huge*!

Shirley looked the length of the horse and groaned inwardly. "If I could just…" she said politely, lifting the horse's mane. Nothing. Shirley took a deep breath as Blazing Star stamped her feet impatiently.

"Good boy – er, girl," Shirley said nervously. Boy! Those feet were massive!

She walked to the other end of the horse. Perhaps under the tail... She reached out gingerly to lift it, but as she did so, Blazing Star flicked her tail out of Shirley's hand. Shirley jumped back quickly, afraid of being kicked. "Easy, Star!" she said. "OK, let's try Plan B, then – I promise I won't touch your tail again." Perhaps the front end was safer, after all!

She wet a cotton wool ball with the contents of a small bottle, and prepared for her next plan of attack.

"What are you doing here?" came a horribly familiar voice.

Uh-oh. Rumbled. It was Bo,

standing watching her, with a frown all over his face.

Shirley didn't stop what she was doing. She didn't want to waste time arguing now! Carefully she rubbed the cotton wool on the mark on Blazing Star's forehead – the distinctive white blaze which had given her her name.

"It won't hurt her," she said casually. "It's just potassium iodide."

Bo walked over. "That's a fifty thousand dollar horse," he said in a tight voice. "It had better *not* hurt her. Otherwise I'll be getting the blame – again!"

He was about to go on, but stopped and stared at the horse's forehead. Blazing Star's blazing star was becoming… a reddish brown colour.

"Her blaze has been put on with

bleach," Shirley explained, wiping the last of it away.

Bo stared at the horse's forehead. "It can't have been!" he exclaimed, shocked at the transformation.

"It has. And she's not Blazing Star," Shirley told him. "Rudy must have switched horses."

CHAPTER 8

Bo's mouth dropped open as the truth hit him. Horse-switching! Although he hated to believe Shirley after all that had happened between them, he couldn't help feeling she was right. There had been something wrong all along.

"She hates liquorice," he said slowly, working it all out for himself. "She doesn't like dogs. And she doesn't like me." It was all falling into place horribly easily.

"It all started to make sense when I found oats in this horse's droppings," Shirley explained. "According to her medical records, the real Blazing Star is allergic to oats. I knew it had to be a different horse." She paused, tentatively stroking the horse's neck. "There's only one thing left to check, before we can be sure."

"What?" asked Bo. His eyes looked sad as he tried to comprehend what had been going on.

"Her registration tattoo," said Shirley. She looked at Bo, challenging him with her eyes.

"That's what you were looking for earlier," Bo realised out loud.

Shirley was rather embarrassed to learn that her nerve-wracking conversation with the horse had been overheard. "You saw…?" she began, tailing off at Bo's nod. "So where is it?" she asked.

Bo hesitated for a second. He knew he could lie about it – or not even tell her, come to that. But…

"What are you going to do – if it is the wrong number, and the wrong horse?" he asked in a low voice.

Then he looked at her, and knew the answer already. They both knew that Shirley would report it to the police straight away, as any good detective should.

"I mean," he said carefully, watching her expression, "are you going to report it before or after the race?"

Shirley paused. "Have you placed your bet?" But she could see by his face that he had. "How much?" she asked.

Bo sighed, and looked down at the ground. "Every cent I've earned," he admitted.

Shirley bit her lip thoughtfully. She realised Bo stood to lose everything if she was right. And, much as she wanted to be right, she didn't want Bo to lose out because of her. No way. He would never forgive her for it – and more to the point, she would never forgive herself.

"Bo…" she started, then stopped, not quite sure what to say to him. This was one decision Bo had to make for himself.

"It's not just the money," he was arguing. "I've known Rudy for years. He just wouldn't do something like this."

But as the words came out of Bo's mouth, he knew there was a hollow ring to them. Only the other day, after all, Rudy had snapped at him in a way that was totally out of character. Maybe he didn't know his friend as well as he thought he had. Maybe...

Bo felt totally torn. He looked at Shirley who – for once – was giving him time to make up his mind, and then at Blazing Star – or whatever her name was. Finally he decided it was no good. Money or no money, he had to do the right thing.

He sighed. Goodbye, winnings, he thought to himself. It was nice nearly knowing you...

"The tattoo's on her lip," he said in the end and, without another glance at Shirley, reached for the halter and grabbed the horse's lip.

"Here..." he said, looking for the numbers.

"What's going on?"

The children turned around to see Rudy standing in the barn door, dressed in his silks for the race. He held an empty canvas bag and was disturbed to find anyone in the barn – particularly Shirley, in her mock-jockey get-up!

"You're not supposed to be here," he told Shirley, not meeting her eye. His voice sounded unusually hard. He crossed to a bench to put a couple of horse brushes in the canvas bag.

Shirley looked quickly over at Bo. Now what?

But Bo was nodding to her. "Go... It's OK," he told her.

Shirley gave him a small good-luck smile, realising that Bo meant to tackle Rudy about the horse-switching, and that he wanted to do it alone. Fair enough, really...

Shirley turned to go – and as she

did so, she spotted something in Rudy's pocket. Sticks of red liquorice! Wait a minute – why would Rudy be giving liquorice to Blazing Star's stand-in? She didn't even like it!

The reality dawned on Shirley as she hurried out of the barn. So, the real Blazing Star had to be around somewhere nearby! With her sharp eyes scanning everything in sight, Shirley moved on quickly in search of the missing horse. Aha! That horse trailer the other side of the paddock looked promising. She ducked under a low fence and strode across to it in a business-like way.

Meanwhile, back in the barn, Bo watched as Rudy took the horse. There was a terrible heavy feeling in the pit of his stomach, as if he was about to sit an exam or go to the dentist.

He was just about to confront his friend with the awful truth, when Rudy spoke first.

"You can't bring your friends around here, you know," he told Bo. "πThe horse belongs to Mrs March, remember, and she doesn't like it…"

Bo interrupted. "Which horse, Rudy?" he said pointedly.

Rudy turned round at the unfriendly note in Bo's voice, and saw from his challenging expression that he had somehow guessed at the truth.

"I can't believe you'd ditch Blazing Star," Bo continued accusingly. "Especially after all your talk about generosity and how you should treat a horse the way you'd treat a friend!"

Rudy couldn't bear the coldness in Bo's eyes. "It's not what you think," he told him apologetically. "Honestly, Bo – it's not what you think."

"Where is she?" Bo demanded.

Rudy was still trying to placate him. "I can't tell you that," he said. "It's for your own good! The less you know the better."

He looked earnestly at Bo. "You've got to trust me, kid."

Bo snorted. "I did trust you, and look what happened! And I'm not a kid, anyway!" He poked at the hay on the ground with his foot, then looked at Rudy once more.

"I'm calling the cops," he told him flatly. Then he turned on his heel and walked stiffly away.

CHAPTER 9

Checking over her shoulder, Shirley approached the horse trailer. She peered in through the gap in the horse trailer door to see… the glossy hindquarters of a chestnut horse. It was wearing exactly the same saddle as the horse they'd just been with.

Shirley held her breath as she clambered, rather ungracefully, into the trailer, and dropped down into the warm straw. She'd be glad when all this messing around with horses was over!

She inched her way along the mare's body, and then was surprised to find herself being nuzzled by a soft nose when she reached the horse's head. Well, this made a change from being kicked at, anyway! Shirley looked up at the horse's face and smiled to see a white star on its forehead.

"Blazing Star," she whispered softly.

Just as she'd expected!

But as she was congratulating herself on her cleverness, she heard a most unwelcome voice outside the trailer.

"I'll get her," it said. It was Tony!

It all happened too quickly for Shirley to be able to do anything other than scramble into the straw. But Tony swung the door open and saw Shirley immediately.

"What are you doing here?" he roared furiously, climbing in after her.

Shirley knew this wasn't exactly going to be a social call. She quickly dodged around the other side of Blazing Star then out of the trailer, jumping to the ground away from the menacing looking stable-hand. Yes! In the clear!

For two seconds, anyway. She ran straight into the arms of Mrs March, who grabbed her.

"Do something with her," Mrs March instructed Tony, pushing Shirley away in disgust.

Tony dragged her off, and Shirley was totally unable to move – or do anything, with his big hand clamped over her mouth. Uh-oh. She was in trouble now, all right.

Within seconds she was bound and gagged, and hidden among hay bales above the stables. While she struggled there, she couldn't believe she was going through all this for a couple of horses! She'd think twice about getting involved with anything equine again!

Shirley struggled against her bonds, but her hands were tied tightly behind her back. Tony had been pretty good on the knots – you had to give it to him. She would be here for a long time at this rate.

Shirley took a few deep breaths and tried to think logically. Struggling and panicking was not going to get her out of this situation! She inched her bottom backwards so that her tied hands were now around her thighs, rather than behind her back. Now if she could just get her feet through her tied hands, too…

Shirley panted and sweated. She wished she'd paid a bit more attention in gym class and worked harder with those stretches. With one last wriggle, though, she was untangled, and her hands were once again in front of her. Quickly she pulled the gag from her mouth and set to work untying the knot around her wrists with her teeth…

Meanwhile, back on the race track, a fanfare sounded. The gate had opened and the race had begun!

"And they're off!" called the track announcer excitedly, and everyone leant forward in their seats as the six racehorses began powering down the track.

Tony and Mrs March looked at

each other. This was it! This could mean some big money for both of them!

"Wicked Widow takes an early lead…" gabbled the announcer, as a slim black horse surged forward, nostrils flaring, hooves pounding. "Paula's Pride is coming up on the inside, and moving through the pack is Blazing Star…"

On his way to the hayloft with Rudy's canvas bag, Bo stopped to listen to the race. Blazing Star was doing well, by all accounts! He crossed his fingers, an anxious frown on his face.

"Coming round the bend, Whistler's Mudder is taking the lead away from Paula's Pride, but look out for Blazing Star, coming up the middle…"

The commentator could hardly get

his words out quick enough. Sure enough, Blazing Star had found a space in the middle and was thundering along, gaining ground all the time on the two other horses in front.

Tony and Mrs March were smiling at each other, both thinking about how much they were going to win. Tony poured out another glass of champagne for each of them. Come on, Blazing Star!

Meanwhile, Bo hurried into the hayloft. He had work to do – and fast! At the same time he started putting the horse brushes away and lifted a saddle on to the rack where it belonged. Elsewhere, at the top of the hayloft, Shirley was shaking the final rope free. Now all she had to do was get down… although one look through the trapdoor almost took her breath away.

It was a very long way down!

But Shirley wasn't stuck for long. She started throwing hay bales down the trapdoor to cushion her fall when she jumped. There was no way she was jumping anywhere without a soft landing!

Bo started in surprise as a hay bale landed almost by his feet. Who was up there in the loft, without a ladder?

He got his answer almost immediately as Shirley, struggling with a heavy bale, slipped and overbalanced. She reached out desperately as she fell through the trapdoor and just managed to grab the edge of it.

Bo looked on in astonishment at the sight of Shirley dangling above the stable floor, clinging on to the edge of the trapdoor with her fingertips.

"Bo!" she yelled in relief when she spotted him. "Help me!"

"Shirley, what are you doing up there?" he asked in amazement.

"It's a long story!" she yelled back, tightening her grip. Then her voice changed with fear. "I'm slipping, Bo! Quick!" she shouted.

Thinking fast, Bo started tossing bales of hay under Shirley. "Hang on," he called. "Hang on just a little bit longer, Shirley!"

Shirley squeezed her eyes shut in fright. Her fingers were getting slippery with sweat and her arms felt as if they were about to pop out of their sockets. She couldn't hang on much longer – she just couldn't. She just...

"Oof!"

She hadn't. Her grip gave way and she dropped from the trapdoor with a scream, landing on the hay – and on top of Bo.

The two of them lay in the hay for a second, slightly stunned.

"You broke my fall," Shirley said quietly, sitting up and coughing on the hay dust.

Bo winced. "I broke something else, too," he said, pretending to click his hand back into place.

They smiled at each other, for the first time in ages.

"Come on," said Bo, standing up and helping Shirley to her feet. "Let's see if we can catch the end of the race. Blazing Star seemed to be doing OK, last I heard."

As they left the hayloft, they could hear the spectators' cheers, and the track announcer's voice over the loudspeaker system. "As they close on the finish line, it's Blazing Star and

Whistler's Mudder!" he was saying, his voice practically cracking with excitement. "And it's Blazing Star at the finish line! Followed by Whistler's Mudder to place, and Paula's Pride to show."

"They won!" cried Bo in excitement. "They did it!" He ran down towards the winners' circle, leaving Shirley no option but to run after him.

At the track-side, Mrs March and Tony were elated too. They were both cheering and hugging each other with delight at their win – but unfortunately their celebrations didn't last long. A tap on the shoulder from a track security officer interrupted them, and as they disentangled themselves, their faces both took on expressions of pure shock. Their brilliant plan didn't seem to have gone quite so brilliantly after all. As another security officer arrived, both Mrs March and Tony started to look more and more downcast.

CHAPTER 10

Bo and Shirley watched as the guilty pair were helped into a police car and driven away.

"You called the police?" Shirley asked in surprise.

"Not me," replied Bo. "Rudy," he added, as Shirley stared at him.

By now, they were at the winners' circle. They went up to Rudy and Blazing Star, just as he was taking off his goggles and giving her a piece of liquorice. People were calling out their congratulations from all around.

"Great race!"

"Brilliantly ridden!"

"You rode the real Blazing Star," Shirley said happily.

"How did you know that?" asked Bo. He didn't think Shirley knew so much about horses to be able to recognise one instantly! Impressive! She must have learned a lot, fast. Unless…

"The liquorice in Rudy's pocket," Shirley pointed out.

Bo smiled to himself. She was just a detective after all. She still didn't know anything about horses!

"Weird horse," Rudy said affectionately, as he scratched Blazing Star's ears.

"So you planned to ride her all along!" Shirley said.

Rudy nodded. "Well, they wanted me to put her back in her stall after the impostor won the race, in case there were any questions." He grinned at Bo. "But we just switched them a little early."

"Mrs March thought Blazing Star was washed up after her tendonitis last year," Bo said, stroking the horse's nose. "But Rudy had faith in you, Star!"

"And you had faith in Rudy," Shirley added.

Bo grinned broadly. "So… wait a minute," he said. "Let me see if I've got this right: you're admitting you were wrong?"

Shirley pursed up her lips. "I wouldn't use the word wrong in this instance, Bo…" she said reprovingly.

Bo laughed out loud. "I don't believe you!" he said. But all the coldness of his voice was long gone, now, and you could tell that there was a part of him that couldn't help admiring Shirley. She was just shameless!

Shirley grinned back, knowing exactly what Bo was thinking. And that was because he was right!

Things went pretty much back to normal after that. Blazing Star went back to her rightful stable, with Rudy hopeful of working for her new owners. Mrs March and Tony faced heavy fines for attempted fraud, and Bo's family managed to pay off a large chunk of their debts with their son's winnings.

Shirley was pleased she had interfered – some good had definitely come from it, although there had been a few sticky moments along the way, particularly between her and Bo.

Back at school, she watched as Bo finished his football practice. He was back in the team once more, too – another result of her detective work, she liked to think. She smiled to herself as she saw him at the bottom of a particularly fierce tackle. Yes, it was definitely worth sticking your neck out for a friend's sake, even if he didn't appreciate it at first!

The coach blew the whistle and Bo hobbled over to Shirley on the sidelines.

"So, does it feel good being back on the team, then?" Shirley couldn't help asking.

Bo rubbed his shoulders and winced in pain. "Mostly," he said, smiling at her.

"So, what did your parents say when you told them how you got the money?" Shirley asked curiously. She knew her dad would have gone ballistic at the word 'gambling', debts or no debts!

Bo shrugged. "Well, first they said thank you."

Shirley could tell there was more to come. "And second?" she encouraged.

Bo pulled a face at her. "Except for football practice, I'm grounded for life!"

Shirley smiled at him as they walked on into the school. OK, OK. So she hadn't got it totally fixed. But hey, great detectives weren't expected to pull off everything, were they?

Who is Shirley Holmes?

THE ESSENTIAL CASE FILE
is the official guide to the exciting
action-adventure TV series.

Inside you will find:
- character profiles
- episode guides
- an introduction to some famous detectives
- amazing detective and crime-solving facts

plus hints, tips and exercises for you to
hone your own powers of observation,
deduction, perception, memory and
imagination!

FROM THE ACTION-ADVENTURE TV SERIES

- ARSON ATTACKS ALL OVER TOWN...
  - A NEW KID IN SCHOOL...
    - A STICKY SITUATION...
      - IS IT ALL TOO HOT TO HANDLE?

Shirley Holmes investigates in:

THE CASE OF THE BURNING BUILDING

Some of Shirley's schoolmates find her odd – Bo Sawchuk, the new kid, certainly does. But when he is accused of starting several fires in the area, proving his innocence becomes more important than avoiding the class weirdo.

Shirley is soon on the case, but realises she will have to convince Bo that the one person he trusts is not as honest as he seems. Her search for the truth puts her in great danger. Only Bo can save her – but will he?

FROM THE ACTION-ADVENTURE TV SERIES

THE ADVENTURES OF Shirley HOLMES

- • A STRING OF DISAPPEARANCES...
- • THREE-TOED FOOTPRINTS IN THE FOREST...
- • BREAK-IN AT THE SCIENCE LAB...
- • UNIDENTIFIABLE FLYING OBJECTS?

Shirley Holmes investigates in:

THE CASE OF THE ALIEN ABDUCTIONS

When three local people claim that they have been abducted by aliens, Shirley's interest is aroused. Her investigations lead her into a world of UFOs, grey extraterrestrials and mysterious implants – where belief is strong, but hard evidence is thin on the ground.

The case seems impossible, especially as there are no apparent links between the victims. Then Shirley's teacher begins acting very strangely. Could Mr Howie be abductee number four...?

FROM THE ACTION-ADVENTURE TV SERIES

- RABBITS AND REPTILES ALL OVER THE PLACE
  - A CLUE IN A VEGGIE BURGER...
    - KIDNAPPING BY NUMBERS...
      - IS THERE MADMAN ON THE LOOSE?

Shirley Holmes investigates in:

THE CASE OF THE DISAPPEARING DRAGON

A break-in at the local pet shop is just the first of a number of strange thefts. Animals are disappearing all over town – some are exotic and expensive, some are household pets and some are so rare they shouldn't even be available to steal!

Shirley is determined to track down the thieves and early clues lead her to suspect the work of the Animal Liberation Front. But, whoever is responsible, just where are they keeping all those animals?

FROM THE ACTION-ADVENTURE TV SERIES

Order Form

To order direct from the publishers, just make a list of the titles you want and fill in the form below:

Name
....

Address
....

....

....

Send to: Dept 6, HarperCollins Publishers Ltd, Westerhill Road, Bishopbriggs, Glasgow G64 2QT.

Please enclose a cheque or postal order to the value of the cover price, plus:

UK & BFPO: Add £1.00 for the first book, and 25p per copy for each additional book ordered.

Overseas and Eire: Add £2.95 service charge. Books will be sent by surface mail but quotes for airmail despatch will be given on request.

A 24-hour telephone ordering service is available to holders of Visa, MasterCard, Amex or Switch cards on 0141-772 2281.

Collins
An *Imprint* of HarperCollins*Publishers*